Are you ready for an adventure in Lo

British Museum

LONDON

Chinatown

St. Paul's Cathedral

Brick Lane

Tower of London

River Thames

Borough Market

London Eye

Big Ben

Tower Bridge

N

W E

S

For a world that
appreciates the uniqueness
of every child

The Adventures in One Dear World

This book belongs to

....

A BIG thank you to all the backers who made this possible!

Ada, Adelaine, Adeola, Adrian, Aggie, Alain, Albert, Alethea, Alexandra, Alice, Alison, Allan, Allison, Alvin, Alvis, Amanda, Amy, Anca, Andrew, Andy, Angela, Anita, Anke, Anna, Anne, Anoop, Aranda, Aris, Artemis, Avril, Ayse, Bandhu, Barbara, Bernadine, Bert, Betty, Billy, Bonnie, Brenda, Bruno, Canace, Candost, Carman, Carmen, Carol, Carrie, Catherine, Cecilia, Celestine, Chiahua, Ching Wah, Chris, Christa, Christina, Cindy, Claire, Claudine, Clementine, Colin, Connie, Cora, Crystal, Cynthia, Daisy, Dana, Darja, David, Davit, Denise, Derek, Diana, Diane, Dimitrios, Dmitriy, Donald, Donna, Eddie, Edmond, Edton, Effie, Effy, Elina, Ella, Elly, Elodie, Emely, Emilio, Emma, Enid, Enrique, Epi, Eric, Ernestina, Estelle, Esther, Eugenia, Eva, Fannie, Fion, Fiona, Fitri, Florence, Francois, Frankie, Freda, Frene, Gabija, Garin, Gary, Genevieve, George, Gigi, Gilbert, Gilles, Glenn, Gokce, Grace, Gregory, Hakon, Harpreet, Harry, Heather, Helen, Heloise, Hilda, Hiwot, HK, Hollie, Hon Lam, Horace, Huei-Shia, Iris, Isabella, Ismail, Jacky, Jacqueline, James, Jane, Janet, Janice, Jason, Jean-Marie, Jeanette, Jenni, Jennifer, Jens-Christian, Jeremy, Jerry, Jess, Jimmy, Jo, Joanie, Joanna, Joanne, Joe, Joey, Johanna, Johnny, Jonathan, Joy, Joyce, Julia, Justin, Kacy, Kamila, Kar Kar, Karman, Karole, Kasuni, Kate, Katherine, Kayin, Ken, Kenneth, Kerstin, Kevin, Kim, Ko Chun, Kon Lim, Koo, Lacie, Lambros, Laurie & Simon, Leo, Lina, Ling, Linh, Lipi, Lorraine, Louise, Lubna, Lucas, Lucy, Luke, Ma Chai, Maggy, Makeba, Marco, Margaret, Maria, Marine, Marise, Marjorie, Mark, Marta, Martin, Martine, Mary, Matilda, Matt, Matteo, Maureen, Mei Kam, Mei Ki, Mei Sum, Melanie, Melinda, Meropi, Michael, Michela, Michelle, Miguel, Mineko, Mirta, Monica, Moon Wing, Nadia, Nadine, Nahas, Naily, Nathalie, Nathan, Nicam, Nick, Nicole, Nidhi, Nilesh, Oi Yan, Olga, Oris, Panayotis, Pancy, Parth, Pat, Patrice, Patrick, Paul, Pei-Ru, Peter, Philippe, Phoebe, Phyllis, Pokee, Pokwang, Praveen, Prudence, Qianni, Rajesh, Rakhee, Raphael, Ray, Rebecca, Rob, Roger, Romain, Roslan, Ruta, Ryan, S.H., Sabine, Sam, Sammi, Samuel, Sandra, Sarah, Saral, Selina, Shelly, Shirley, Simon, Sindy, Siyuan, SK, Sofia, Sofie, Solveig , Sophie, Stelios, Steve, Susanna, Svenja, Sylvie, TKHLLM&m, Tammy, Tania, Terence, Thi Ri, Thomas, Tim, Tony, Tracy, Trang, Trevor, Ulrike, Valentin, Van, Vanguelis, Vassili, Veronica, Vicky, Vilyana, Vivian, Voon Fui, Wai Yen, Wan Si Fung, Xin Wei, Yancy, Yasmin, Yasser, Yating, Yeung Yeung, Yin, Yujia, Yvette, Zack, Zhizhi, Zohasina and everybody (especially my husband Rafael!) who has supported me along the way!

I would also like to thank the following people and organisations for their permission to reproduce material on the following pages:

Front cover and various pages: my lovely mum Connie Yu, p7: J Brew/Flickr, p11-12: The London Eye Company Limited, p16: Sean MacEntree/Flickr (CC BY 2.0), p18: Robertsharp and Angel Ganev/Flickr (CC BY 2.0), p20: JeepersMedia and Link Humans UK/Flickr (CC BY 2.0), p21: Janice Watson Photography and Grant Cherrington/Flickr (CC BY 2.0), p23: Sumit/Flickr CC BY 2.0, Deepraj/Wikimedia Commons (CC BY 2.5).

Every effort has been made to trace and acknowledge the ownership of copyright. If any rights have been omitted, the publisher offers to rectify this in any future editions following notification.

Printed in China. First Edition 2017 by One Dear World Ltd, Kemp House, 152 City Road, London EC1V 2NX

ISBN 978-1-9998200-0-8

The Adventures in One Dear World

LONDON HAT HUNTING MISSION

Winnie Mak Tselikas

One Dear World

London is a city of diversity, where five little people live.

Hope loves animals and likes the city farm in the capital.

Mudchute Park & Farm

Jun likes to play ball and aims at the wall.

Southbank Centre

2

Parth likes to travel on the bus, where sitting on top deck is a must.

Bus ride over the River Thames

Lea likes to ask why and dreams of flying high.

Beautiful view of London

3

Their best friend is **Mr. Globe.**

He is mostly happy, sometimes cheeky and rarely grumpy!

They are good friends living in the same town and they often play together in the park. Then, one day...

... Mr. Globe falls ill.

"Mr. Globe, how do you feel?" asks Jun worriedly.

Mr. Globe says, "I have a **BAD** headache, but there is a cure. Go to the **British Museum**'s library and you will find a book called *"HEAD AID for the Globe"*."

As they arrive at the library, they start searching.

Jun says, "Running **up** here is fun!"

Hope says, "Let me look on the **left**!"

Lea says, "I'll go on the **right**!"

Parth says, "I'll look for it **down** here then."

Finally, they find the book in a hidden corner and it says ...

For a painful head,
You need magic hats.
Collect a large pile and
They'll be of great help.

While Hope, Lea and Jun are talking about the hats they have in mind, Parth has an idea!

"Mr. Globe once said that London is full of surprises. We can travel around London to find the magic hats!" he says excitedly.

"Follow me down to the Tube! I know a place that has got the best view of London," says Parth as he leads the rest of them into the Tube station.

"Hey, did you know this **London Tube** line is the oldest in the world?" asks Lea.

"How old is it?" Hope wonders aloud.

"I know! It's more than 150 years old!" answers Jun.

"See the big wheel in the sky?" asks Jun.

"Yes, it means we are at the **London Eye**," replies Lea.

"Will we see any magic hats up there?" says Hope.

"Sure, let's go!" says Parth.

KEEP LONDON

"Wow! I can see far, far away!" says Jun.

"Oh yes, the cars and people look so small down there," says Hope.

As they go up the **London Eye**, they hear **Big Ben** on the other side of the River Thames starting to chime.

"Let's work out where we should go next," says Parth.

BING!

BONG!!

Their first stop is at **Buckingham Palace**.

"This is home of the Royal Family, isn't it?" asks Jun.

"Yes, playing hide and seek here must be fun!" says Hope.

Parth and Lea think the soft *bearskin hat* on the Royal Guard can ease Mr. Globe's headache. So they wait at the gate with all other tourists and show a banner during the Changing of the Guard.

Can you help Mr. Globe?

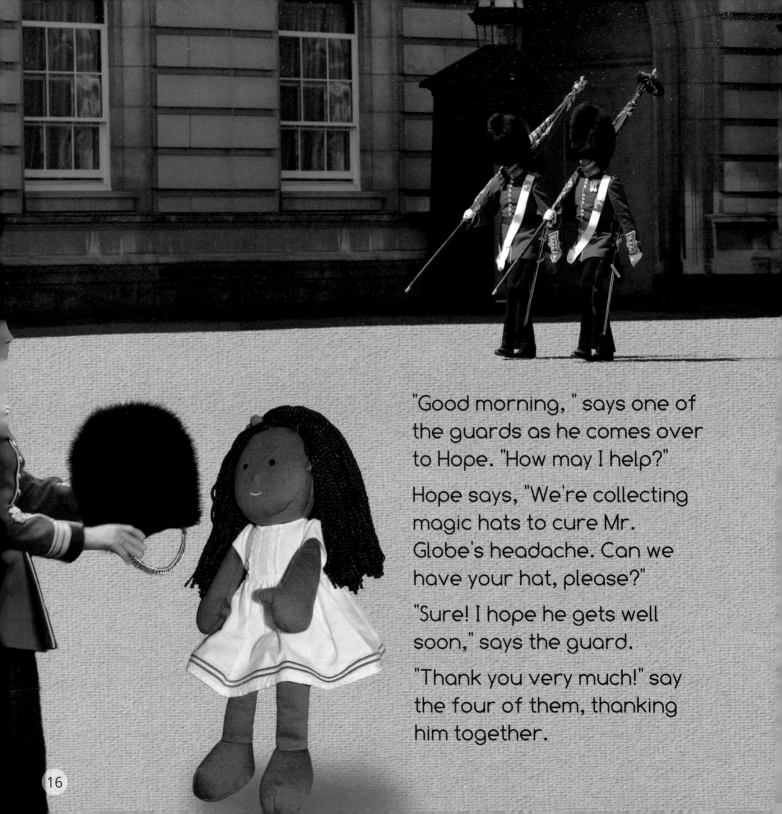

"Good morning, " says one of the guards as he comes over to Hope. "How may I help?"

Hope says, "We're collecting magic hats to cure Mr. Globe's headache. Can we have your hat, please?"

"Sure! I hope he gets well soon," says the guard.

"Thank you very much!" say the four of them, thanking him together.

Next, the four of them go to **South Kensington** to get a *beret* and they even learn how to say "thank you" in French.

"Merci beaucoup!" says Jun, as he is having a croissant.

Then they go to **Portobello Road** where a carnival is held every summer. They get a *rasta tam* from a Jamaican drummer.

"Tank yuh," says Lea in Jamaican.

18

Next stop is **Edgware Road**. There are many Middle Eastern restaurants and cafes on the road. There they find a *fez* in a shop.

"شكرا (shukran)," says Parth in Arabic, while enjoying a baklawa.

When they reach 221b **Baker Street**, home of the famous detective Sherlock Holmes, not only does Jun find a *deer stalker*, but also a pipe and a magnifying glass.

"Elementary!" says Jun.

As they arrive at **Chinatown**, they find a *Manchu Princess hat* and a *melon cap* which Chinese people wore back in the Qing dynasty in the 18th century.

"谢谢你 **(xie xie ni)**," says Lea in Mandarin.

Then they pass by **St. Paul's Cathedral** and see a couple who have just got married, so they get a *fascinator* and a *top hat* from the guests.

"Congratulations!" says Hope.

ST. PAUL'S CHURCHYARD EC4
CITY OF LONDON

Their last stop is **Brick Lane**. The area is rich in South Asian culture. There they find a supermarket with different types of rice, spices and herbs. There is also a store selling a beautiful collection of hats.

"Which one should we choose for Mr. Globe? asks Lea, while eating a spicy samosa.

"Let's bring these different *turbans* and all other hats here to him!" suggests Parth.

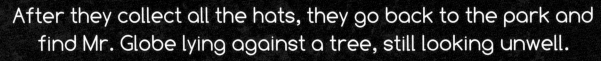

After they collect all the hats, they go back to the park and find Mr. Globe lying against a tree, still looking unwell.

Mr. Globe looks at all the hats and says, "I am so glad to see you all. Thank you for bringing all these hats."

As he puts on each hat, he begins to look better.

After Mr. Globe puts on all the hats, it starts to rain heavily.
Everybody runs hand in hand through the rain.

Finally, they find a shelter to stay dry.

"Let's wait here until the rain stops," suggests Mr. Globe.

At last, the rain stops and a rainbow appears. At the same time, a seedling pops out of Mr. Globe's head.

"Thank you so much dear friends. After putting on all these different hats, I feel complete and alive now." says Mr. Globe.

"Mission accomplished!" says Hope.

"We are now ready for our next colourful adventure!"

I got invited to the Finnish Sauna #slowfinland

A Note From the Author

The creation of One Dear World multicultural dolls and storybook wouldn't be possible without your support.

It started with an idea of bringing my son Alex some dolls and a story where everybody celebrates their differences. Inspired by the multicultural environment in London, I wanted to show children around the world how culturally diverse London is through the dolls' adventure and how children with different cultures can work together in harmony.

The introduction of visually appealing hats is intended to be an entry point for parents to talk about different cultures, which can sometimes be abstract, at home.

Thank you for allowing me the privilege to bring these dolls and their story to life.

Winnie Mak Tselikas

P.S. Which city do you think the dolls should go next? Let us know through our social media channels @onedearworld!

Hat Hunt Map

Portobello Road

Edgware Road

Baker Street

Marble Arch

Buckingham Palac

South Kensington